Benjamin Hobson

A Medical Vocabulary in English and Chinese

Anatiposi

Benjamin Hobson

A Medical Vocabulary in English and Chinese

Reprint of the original, first published in 1858.

1st Edition 2023 | ISBN: 978-3-38233-520-5

Anatiposi Verlag is an imprint of Outlook Verlagsgesellschaft mbH.

Verlag (Publisher): Outlook Verlag GmbH, Zeilweg 44, 60439 Frankfurt, Deutschland
Vertretungsberechtigt (Authorized to represent): E. Roepke, Zeilweg 44, 60439 Frankfurt, Deutschland
Druck (Print): Books on Demand GmbH, In de Tarpen 42, 22848 Norderstedt, Deutschland

A

MEDICAL VOCABULARY

IN.

ENGLISH AND CHINESE.

———◆◆——

BY

BENJ. HOBSON M. B. LOND.

OF THE

. LONDON MISSIONARY SOCIETY.

———◆◆——

SHANGHAE MISSION PRESS:
1858.

VOCABULARY

OF TERMS USED IN ANATOMY,

MEDICINE, MATERIA MEDICA,

AND NATURAL PHILOSOPHY, &c.

醫學英華字釋

ANATOMY AND PHYSIOLOGY.

全體部位功用

THE OSSEOUS SYSTEM. 全體之骨

The skeleton.	交連全體之骨
The shape or form of bones.	骨骼之形
The shaft or body.	骨之中端
The superior extremity.	骨之上端
The inferior extremity.	骨之下端
The anterior and posterior surface.	骨前後面
Long and short bones.	骨之長短
Round and flat bones.	圓骨扁骨
Thick and thin bones.	厚骨薄骨
Their smooth or rough surface.	骨面滑滯
Their structure hard or pliable.	骨質堅嫩
Their form straight or crooked.	骨形直曲

Their structure open or condensed.	骨質疏緊
The external surface of bone.	骨之外面
The medullary canal.	骨之髓路
Bony eminences and depressions.	骨凸骨凹
Tuberosity or angle.	骨之稜角
Spine or crust.	骨之廉
Foramina or holes.	骨之孔穴
Styloid processes.	骨之銳者
Periosteum or covering.	骨衣
Attachment of muscles.	肉筋相連處
Uses of the bones.	骨之功用
To protect organs.	骨保護功用
To support the frame.	骨扶持功用
For prehension and motion.	骨把握運動功用
Bones of the head.	頭骨
Occipital bone.	枕骨
Parietal bone.	左右臚頂骨
Frontal bone.	額骨
Temporal bone.	耳門骨
Sphenoid bone.	蝴蝶骨
Ethmoid bone.	鼻中上水泡骨
Vertebral column.	脊骨
Cervical vertebræ.	脊頸骨七節
Axis and atlas.	頸骨首節次節
Dorsal vertebræ.	脊背骨十二節
Lumbar vertebræ.	腰骨五節
Sacrum.	尾骶骨
Os coccyx.	尾閭骨
Bones of the face.	面骨
Nasal bone.	鼻梁骨

Superior jaw bone.	上牙床骨
Inferior jaw bone.	下牙床骨
Malar or cheek bone.	顴骨
Lachrymal bone.	淚管骨
Palate bone.	上腭後甲鐘骨
Turbinated bone.	鼻中下水泡骨
The vomer.	犂頭骨
Sutures of the skull.	髑髏衚接之縫
Superior region or summit.	髑髏之頂
Inferior region or base.	髑髏之底
Temporal region.	太陽穴
Inner and outer table.	髑髏骨內片外片
Orbits right and left.	左右眼窠
Nasal fossæ or nostrils.	鼻孔左右
Anterior and posterior.	鼻孔前後
Incisor and canine teeth.	門牙貳牙
Small and large molar.	顋牙大牙
Temporary or milk teeth.	小兒乳牙
Permanent teeth.	大人不換之牙
Alveoli or sockets.	牙槽
Crown and fang of teeth.	牙面牙齦
Os hyoides or tongue bone.	舌根骨
The thorax or chest	胸膛
Sternum or breast bone.	胸骨
Ensiform cartilage.	胸下脆骨
Ribs.	脅骨左右各十二支
Costal cartilages.	脅脆骨
Clavicle or collar bone.	鎖柱骨
Scapula or shoulder bone.	飯匙骨即肩髀骨
Humerus or arm bone.	上臂骨

Ulna or fore-arm bone.	正肘骨
Radius or turning hand bone.	輔肘骨
Carpus or wrist bones.	腕骨
Metacarpal or hand bones.	掌骨
Phalanges or finger bones.	揩骨
Pelvis.	尻骨盤
Os innominatum or unnamed bone.	胯骨
Ischium or sitting bone.	坐骨卽臀骨
The symphisis pubis.	骨盤橫骨交縫
The acetabulum.	胯骨白
Femur or thigh bone.	大腿骨
Tibia or leg bone.	小腿骨
Fibula or auxiliary bone.	輔腿骨
Patella or knee-pan.	膝蓋骨
Os calcis or ankle bone.	脚交節骨
Astralagus or heel bone.	脚跟骨
Metatarsal or foot bones.	脚掌前後骨
Phalanges or toe bones.	脚趾骨

ARTICULATIONS.	全體交節

Moveable and immoveable joints.	交節有動有不動
Shoulder joint.	肩髆交節
Elbow joint.	臂肘交節
Wrist joint.	手腕交節
Hip joint.	大腿交節
Knee joint.	膝凹交節
Ankle joint.	腿脚交節
Articulation of the jaw.	下牙床骨交節
Do.　　of the spine.	脊骨各節交節

Cartilage.	脆骨
Flat and round ligaments.	夋節扁筋圓筋
Synovial membrane.	夋節夾膜
Synovia or joint oil.	夾膜脂膏
The use or action of joints.	夋節功用
Flexion and extension.	伸縮功用
Rotary motion.	運動功用
Rotation of the arm and leg.	臂腿運轉
Flexion or bending of the arm.	臂收縮
Extension of the arm and hand.	臂手伸直
Bending in of the fingers.	手指曲握
Adduction of the arm.	大臂收縮
Abduction of the leg.	腿外放
Flexion and extension of the foot.	足夋節伸縮
Turning of the head to either side.	頭左右轉動
Bending of head forwards or backwards.	頭俯頭仰
Ball and socket joint.	杵臼夋節

THE MUSCLES. 各處肌肉

Muscles of the head and neck.	頭頸肌肉
Do. of the abdomen.	肚腹肌肉
Do. of the chest.	胸腔肌肉
Do. of the back.	背肌肉
Do. of the hand and foot.	手足肌肉
Do. of the senses.	五官肌肉
Diaphragm.	膈肉
The form of muscles.	諸肉之形
Large and small size.	大小肌肉
Round and broad muscles.	圓肉扁肉

Thick and thin muscles.	厚肉薄肉
Opposite pairs.	肌肉對偶
Expansion and contraction of muscles.	肌肉舒縮功用
Their bony attachment.	肉骨相連之處
Their two extremities.	肉兩端
The tendons.	肉筋
Round and flat tendons.	圓筋扁筋
Investing membrane of muscles.	肌肉胞膜
Fatty tissue.	肌肉肥網
Muscular force.	肉之力
Muscular action in walking.	肉行動功用
Do. in sitting and rising.	肉坐立功用
Do. in leaping and swimming.	肉跳躍洑水功用
Turning motion of the hand.	肉轉動手功用
Combined and opposite action.	肉合用對用
The muscles of expression.	呈露七情之肉
The voluntary and involuntary muscles.	自主不自主兩種肉
The sphincter muscles.	歛縮口門之肉
Blood-vessels and nerves.	肉中血管腦氣筋

The Circulating Organs. 運行血之器

The heart.	心 —— sum
Arteries or pulsating vessels.	血脈管
Veins or returning blood vessels.	廻血管
Capillaries or very minute vessels.	微絲血管
The arterial system.	血脈大小管
Aorta or great artery.	總脈管
Pulmonary artery.	心肺廻血總管
...e arch of the aorta.	總脈管栱

The chief branches of the aorta.	總脈管大支
The left and right carotids.	頸左右脈管
Their (principal) branches.	頸脈管分支
Tracheal artery.	喉脈管
Lingual artery.	舌脈管
Facial artery.	面唇脈管
Occipital artery.	頭後脈管
Temporal artery.	太陽穴脈管
Maxillary artery.	上牙床骨脈管
Anterior & posterior cerebral arteries.	腦體前後脈管
Opthalmic artery.	眼脈管
Subclavian artery right and left.	入臂左右脈管
Brachial artery.	上臂脈管
Radial and ulnar.	下臂內外脈管
Palmar arch.	手心脈管之栱
Arteries of the fingers.	手指內外脈管
Thoracic aorta.	膈肉以上總脈管
Abdominal aorta.	膈肉以下總脈管
Intercostal branches.	脊骨脈管左右支
Gastric or artery of the stomach.	胃脈管
Hepatic or artery of the liver.	肝脈管
Artery of the spleen.	脾脈管
Superior and inferior mesenteric.	小腸大腸脈管
Renal or kidney arteries.	內腎脈管
The iliac arteries.	小腹左右大脈管
The iliac or pelvic branches.	小腹左右脈管之支
Femoral or artery of the thigh.	大腿脈管
Popliteal or artery of the knee.	膝凹脈管
Anterior tibial artery.	小腿前脈管
Posterior tibial artery.	小腿後脈管

8

Deep and superficial branches of foot.	足淺深脈管
Muscular branches.	入肉脈管各處大小支
Anastamosing branches.	脈管相通小支

THE VENOUS SYSTEM. 廻血大小管

Superior vena cava or great vein.	上廻血總管
Inferior vena cava or great vein.	下廻血總管
Pulmonary veins.	肺心廻血管
Veins of the head and neck.	頭頸廻血管
Veins of the arm.	臂手廻血管
Veins of the leg.	腿足廻血管
Veins of the abdominal viscera.	肚腹內廻血管
Valves of the veins.	廻血管之門
Coats of the blood-vessels.	血管之體三層

The lymphatics or absorbents.	吸液各管
The thoracic duct.	吸液總管
The lymphatics of the head and neck.	頭頸吸液管
Do. of the upper and lower extremities.	手足吸液管
The lymphatics of the viscera.	內部吸液管
The lymphatics of the mesentery.	腸膜吸液管
The mesenteric glands.	腸膜核粒
The lymphatic glands of the neck.	頸核粒
The glands of the groin.	腿腹相連之處核粒
The glands of the axilla.	腋核粒

THE NERVOUS SYSTEM. 腦體腦髓腦筋體用

| Cerebrum or large brain. | 大腦之體 |
| The general form of the brain. | 腦之形 |

The investing membranes.	腦胞三層
Dura mater or outer membrane.	腦之外胞膜
Arachnoid or double investing ditto.	腦胅膜
Pia mater or inner investing ditto.	腦之內胞膜
The summit and base of the brain.	腦頂腦底
The size of the brain.	腦體比較或大或小
The weight of the brain.	腦體重輕
The consistence of the brain.	腦質堅軟
The external convolutions.	腦外面淺深盤曲之綯
The anterior and posterior fissure.	腦前後縫
The two hemispheres.	腦左右兩枚
Anterior middle and posterior lobes.	腦前中後葉
Horizontal and vertical section.	腦橫割直割所見
White and grey matter.	腦白色灰色
Great commissure or connecting fibres.	兩枚中相連之絲
The lateral ventricles.	腦左右大房
Anterior middle and posterior cornua.	大房前中後角形
The small ventricles.	兩小房
The cerebellum or little brain.	小腦
Two lateral lobes.	小腦左右兩枚
Internal pinnated leaf appearance.	小腦橫割綯紋似葉
Medulla oblongata or head of spinal cord.	大腦小腦之蒂即髓頭
The spinal cord or marrow.	脊骨髓
The investing membranes of the cord.	脊髓內外胞膜
Anterior and posterior fissure.	脊髓前後縫
Appearance of a cross section.	橫割脊髓所見
Grey and white matter.	脊髓灰白色
Anterior and posterior columns.	脊髓前後兩柱
Anterior column or seat of motion.	前柱運動功用
Posterior column or seat of sensation	後柱知覺功用

B

Cranial nerves, nine pairs.	左右腦氣筋九對
1st pair or olfactory nerve.	第一對入鼻孔司顙
2nd pair or optic nerve	第二對入眼司見
3rd pair or motor nerve of the eyelid.	第三對運眼上胞
4th pair or motor nerve of oblique muscles.	第四對運轉眼肉
5th pair or great sensitive nerve of head and face.	第五對入頭面司知覺
6th pair or motor nerve to the eye.	第六對入眼直肉
7th pair or motor nerve of head and face.	第七對入頭面司運動
The second branch or auditory nerve.	第七對又一支入耳司聽
8th pair or pneumogastric nerve.	第八對入心肺胃
9th pair or lingual nerve.	第九對運動舌
Spinal nerves—31 pairs.	左右髓筋三十一對
Their anterior and posterior roots.	髓筋前後根
Anterior or motor root.	前根運動功用
Posterior or sensitory root.	後根知覺功用
The two roots unite & make one nerve.	兩根合爲一筋
Eight pairs distributed to the arm.	八對分入全臂
Twelve pairs to chest and abdomen.	十二對分佈胸腹
Five pairs to front part of thigh and leg.	五對入小腹及腿足前
Six pairs to back part of thigh and leg.	六對分佈腿足後
The many knotted or sympathetic nerve.	臟腑百節筋
The brain is the instrument of the soul.	腦爲靈性之機
The source of sensation.	腦知覺之原
The ruler of the entire body.	腦爲百體之主
The hands and feet are its servants.	手足爲腦之使
The senses are its inlets or doors.	五官爲腦之門戶
Brain, cord, and nerves are all connected	腦髓筋三種相連互應
No place is destitute of nerves.	腦氣筋無處不到
Their reflex action.	傳遞往來知覺運動

...rvous influence is unceasing in ...s operation.	腦髓之氣功用不息
...e action produces convulsion.	腦力妄用爲癇
...of nervous power is paralysis.	腦力失爲癱瘓

THE SENSE OF SIGHT. 眼官體用

...ye.	眼目
...yeball.	眼球
...yebrows.	眼眉 *ngán mee*
...r and lower eyelids.	眼上下胞
...ular or closing muscle of the eye.	上下胞圓紋閉目肉
...levator of the eyelid.	上胞直紋開目肉
...yelashes.	眼睫毛
...l cartilages.	睫邊上下脆骨
...arsal follicles.	兩瞼津液管
...al and external canthus	內外眦
...icula.	內眦肉
...ymal apparatus.	生淚之器
...ymal gland.	淚核
...a or lachrymal openings.	內眦上下小孔
...ymal ducts.	淚上下管
...ymal sac.	淚囊
...canal.	入鼻淚管
...nctiva of the eye and eyelid.	罩睛皮卽眼胞內皮
...ornea.	明角罩
...clerotic coat.	眼白殼
...horoid or vascular membrane.	血絡黑油衣
...etina or nervous membrane.	腦筋衣
...ptic nerve or cord.	眼系
...ris.	眼簾

The ciliary processes.	眼簾摺紋
The pupil.	瞳人
The crystalline lens.	睛珠
Its capsule or coat.	睛珠衣
Anterior chamber.	前房
Posterior chamber.	後房
Aqueous humour.	前後房水
Vitreous humour.	大房水
Hyaloid or transparent membrane.	大房內箔明衣
The muscles of the eyeball.	牽眼球肉
A cushion of fat in the orbit.	眼窠內肥網墊
Blood-vessels and nerves of the eye.	眼中血管腦氣筋
The wonderful function of the eye.	眼官功用極奧妙
The eye is the most important sense.	眼爲最要之官
Both eyes act simultaneously.	兩眼功用互應
No difference in structure or function.	兩眼體用無別
They are protected in front by the eye-lashes and lids.	眼胞睫毛在前保護
Around and behind by the orbits.	眼窠保護眼球周圍
Their movements are rapid and inappreciable.	眼動靈活人自不覺
The eye is round like a ball.	眼圓如球
The eye and light are mutually adapted.	眼與光相合而有見
Can perceive distant and near objects.	眼能遠近皆見
Can see minute as well as large objects.	眼能小大皆見
Can distinguish form and colour.	眼能分別形色
It informs the mind of the outer world.	眼能令知外事
Can accommodate itself to strong and feeble light.	眼能依光力大小合用
The iris or curtain protects the retina.	眼隔簾保護腦筋衣
The pupil dilates or contracts according to the light.	瞳人展縮以合光力

The colour of the iris varies in men.	人眼簾色不同
Light travels in straight lines.	光直射不曲
Passing through convex glasses, it is brought to a focus.	光透過凸鏡收聚
Through concave glasses, the opposite.	光透過凹鏡展開
The cornea is transparent and convex like a watch-glass.	明角罩明凸如錶蓋
The humours of the eye are perfectly limpid.	眼前後房水極清
The crystalline lens is clear and convex.	睛珠明淨而凸
Rays of light must enter the pupil to become visible.	光射入瞳人始能見
Passing the cornea and humours, they suffer refraction.	光入罩經睛水而收束
The image or object is painted on the retina.	光影映於腦筋衣如畫
The optic nerve transmits its impression to the brain.	腦筋傳物影至腦而見
The image is always inverted in the eye.	物影至眼底倒轉
The farther the object, the smaller its image.	眼見物愈遠影愈小
The nearer the object, the larger its image.	眼見物愈近影愈大
The image in each eye is blended into one.	兩眼二影合爲一
Eyes out of axis have double vision.	目斜者見物一形一影
The black pigment absorbs all the light.	黑油衣接光色不令返
The blacker the pupil, the clearer the vision.	瞳人愈黑視愈明
The more lively it moves, the better the sight.	瞳人愈靈動視愈明
Vision is affected by the slightest injury.	視官一處病則不明
A little opacity of the cornea renders it defective.	明角罩署昏則視不明
Too much convexity causes near-sightedness.	明角罩太凸不能見遠
Want of convexity, far-sightedness.	明角罩平不能見近
Convex glasses can rectify flat eyes.	凸鏡能治明角罩平

Concave glasses, prominent ones.	凹鏡能治明角罩凸
Sight neither strong nor weak suits vision best.	光不濃不淡合視官
The eye and ear mutually assist each other.	眼耳交相助
The eye guides the hand and foot.	眼引導手足而有用
In the embryo the eye is first formed.	胎中兒最初有眼
But who can declare how?	此奧妙誰能解

THE SENSE OF HEARING. 耳官體用

The ear.	耳
The pinna or lobe of the ear.	耳外輪
The cartilage of the ear.	耳輪脆骨
The auditory canal.	耳外孔卽耳外竅
The wax of the ear.	耳膩
The middle ear or tympanum.	耳中竅
The membrane of the tympanum.	耳中竅膜卽內皮
The eustachian tube.	中竅通喉氣管
The small bones of the ear.	耳中四小骨
The small muscles of the ear.	耳中小肉
The internal ear or vestibule.	耳內竅
The semicircular canals.	內竅半圈骨管
Cochlea or spiral passages.	螺紋骨
The organ is safely encased in bone.	耳管周圍有骨包固
The delicate membrane of the inner ear.	內竅薄膜
The limpid fluid of the inner ear.	內竅清水
The auditory or hearing nerve.	內竅腦氣筋
The external ear collects the sound.	外竅接聲音
The air of the middle ear transmits it.	中竅之氣傳聲音
The small bones also do the same.	中竅四小骨亦傳聲音

The nervous filaments of the inner ear receive it.	內竅腦筋如網接聲音
The nerve transmits the same to the brain.	總腦筋傳聲於腦而能聽
The ear can distinguish the intensity of sound.	耳官能聽大小聲音
Can distinguish its distance.	耳官能聽遠近聲音
Can distinguish the most delicate tones.	耳官能分別八音
It instantly transmits them.	耳竅傳聲最速
Man's sense of hearing more perfect than that of animals.	人耳機妙過禽獸
Obstruction of the outer ear interferes with hearing.	外中塞則聲不傳而聾
Disease of the middle ear occasions deafness.	中竅有病傳聲不靈
Disease of the nerve, entire loss of hearing.	內竅腦氣筋壞則不能聽
Sound is produced by vibration of the air.	空氣搖動而爲聲
The more rapid the vibration, the more acute the sound.	氣搖動愈速聲愈高
The more slow, the more grave.	氣搖動愈緩聲愈底
Solids transmits sounds the best.	物質堅則傳聲至遠
Fluids and gases more slowly.	水與氣傳聲遞緩

THE SENSE OF TASTE. 口舌之官體用

The tip of the tongue.	舌之尖
The surface of the tongue.	舌之面
Papillæ of the tongue.	舌面尖粒
The frænum or cord of the tongue.	舌底筋帶
Several muscles unite to form the tongue.	數肉合而成舌
Its root is attached to bone.	舌根與骨相連
The muscles by their action move the tongue.	肉伸縮搖動舌

The motion is so quick as to be unperceived.	舌極靈捷不自覺
Salivary glands keep the mouth moist.	六核生水潤口舌
A dry tongue loses the power of taste.	舌乾則不知味
The nerves of the tongue are numerous.	舌膈腦氣筋最多
The tongue distinguishes every taste.	舌分別各味
Each substance has its own taste.	各物皆有本味
Tastes are pungent and insipid.	味有濃淡
Sweet, acrid, bitter, and salt.	味有甘苦辛鹹
If taste is lost there is no appetite.	口不知味則不思食
Children dislike strong flavours.	小兒不喜濃味
The aged take delight in them.	老人喜濃味
Taste and smell are closely connected.	舌與鼻夌相助

THE SENSE OF SMELL. 鼻官功用

The nose is in the middle of the face.	鼻居面中
The bridge of the nose.	鼻梁
The tip of the nose.	鼻準
The cartilages.	鼻脆骨
The external openings.	鼻外孔
Separated by bone into two halves.	鼻隔骨分左右
The anterior and posterior nostrils.	鼻前孔後孔
The lining membrane.	鼻內皮
Nerves ramify upon it.	腦筋分佈鼻內皮
The olfactory branches are many.	鼻腦筋支最多
The nose distinguishes odours.	鼻能別臭美惡
Each odoriferous body has its own smell.	物香者皆有本臭
Their vehicle is the air.	臭至鼻皆氣所傳
Dryness of secretion occasions loss of smell.	鼻乾不覺臭

The larger the surface, the keener the sense.	鼻竅寬大聞愈靈
This sense in animals is superior to man.	獸聞官靈於人
Odours are weak and strong.	臭有濃淡
Pleasant and disgusting.	臭有美惡
Infants have scarcely any smell.	嬰兒聞官不靈
The aged have a keen sense of smell.	老人聞官愈靈
Fragrant odours refresh the spirits.	臭美補精神
Disgusting ones destroy the appetite.	臭惡令胃不欲食

THE SENSE OF TOUCH. 手知覺功用

The fingers are the chief sense of touch.	手指知覺最靈
Can take the place of sight.	手知覺能代眼目
This faculty improves on exercise.	手知覺愈用愈靈
The blind can read by their fingers.	盲者以手讀凸字書
By them the form &c. of bodies is known.	手辨物之形質寒熱
The human hand is a wonderful instrument.	手爲最靈之器
The finger ends are best supplied with nerves.	指端腦氣筋最多
This sense is imperfect in infancy and old age.	老幼人手知覺不靈

THE ORGANS OF DIGESTION. 消化飲食之器

The alimentary canal.	飲食經過之路
A lining membrane connects the whole.	腸胃內皮與口相連
The mouth.	口
The pharynx or gullet.	喉嚨
Œsophagus.	食管
The abdominal viscera.	膈下臟腑

Stomach.	胃
Small intestines.	小腸
Large intestines.	大腸
Liver.	肝
Pancreas or sweet-bread.	甜肉
Spleen.	脾
Each organ from mouth downwards.	口至肛門各部位
The boundaries of the mouth.	口之界
Before are the lips and teeth.	口前爲唇爲牙
The roof is the palate.	口之上爲膞
The sides the cheeks.	口之左右爲腮
The tongue its floor.	舌爲口底
Behind is the curtain or soft palate.	口後隔簾卽喉肉
Its inferior border the uvula.	隔簾下界卽吊鐘
The tonsils.	隔簾後左右之核
Parotid glands.	耳下生水之核
Submaxillary glands.	牙床骨下生水之核
Sublingual glands.	舌底生水之核
Seven openings of the pharynx.	喉嚨七孔
Communicates above with the nostrils.	上通鼻孔
On either side with the eustachian tube.	左右通耳
With the mouth in front.	前通口
With the trachea below.	下通氣管
Inferiorly with the œsophagus.	更下連食管
Its cross and longitudinal muscles.	食管肉直紋橫紋
Œsophagus is behind the trachea.	食管在氣管後
Is in front of the vertebræ.	食管在頸脊骨前
Passes through the diaphragm to the stomach.	食管經過膈肉入胃
The stomach is beneath and on the left side.	胃居膈下之左

Its cardiac orifice.	胃上口名賁門
Its form as a curved bag.	胃形紆曲如袋
Its left part the largest.	胃左端大過右端
Inferior mouth or pylorus.	胃下口名幽門
Omentum on its inferior border.	胃肥網在下界
The three coats of the stomach.	胃有三層
The middle or muscular coat.	中層肉紋斜交
The inner or villous coat	內層皮紋摺疊
The outer or peritoneal coat.	外層即肚腹胞膜
The boundaries of the stomach.	胃之界
The diaphragm above.	膈肉在胃上
The spleen on the left.	脾居胃左
The liver on the right.	肝居胃右
The transverse colon below.	胃下爲大腸中廻
The pancreas behind	甜肉在胃後
And wall of the abdomen in front.	肚肉脊骨在胃前
The intestinal canal.	小腸大腸之路
The duodenum or curved part.	小腸頭曲處
It touches the gall-bladder in front.	肝膽居其前
Receives the biliary and pancreatic ducts.	曲處接膽管甜肉管
Small intestines are long and convoluted.	小腸長而廻曲
They open into the large intestines.	小腸下口入大腸
The mesentery connects them with the spine.	小大腸胞膜粘連脊骨
In its folds are many blood-vessels and lacteals.	膜間多血管吸液管
Ascending, transverse, and descending colon.	大腸分上中下三廻
The cæcum is in the right iliac fossa.	大腸頭在肚腹右下
Its worm-like appendage.	上廻小頭如蚓尾
Ascending colon has the right kidney behind it.	上廻後當右內腎
In front is the abdominal wall.	上廻前當肚腹

Transverse part is in contact with liver and stomach.	中廻橫當肝胃之下
From the spleen downwards is the descending colon.	下廻自脾位直下
Curved portion or sigmoid flexure.	下廻至胯骨邪曲
The rectum or straight intestine.	曲處之下名直腸
Behind is the sacrum.	直腸在尾骶骨前
Before the bladder.	直腸在膀胱後
Intestines have 3 coats like the stomach.	小大腸皮有三層
The liver is the largest of the viscera	肝在臟腑中體最大
Is suspended by four ligaments.	肝有四筋帶繫挂
Superior surface smooth and convex.	上界外面圓凸而滑
Divided into right and left lobes.	肝分左右葉
The right considerably larger.	右葉大過左葉
Inner surface irregularly concave.	肝內面凸凹不平
Inferior border is thin and sharp.	肝下界扁薄而銳
Colour of the liver is deep red.	肝色紫
Its substance is dense and heavy.	肝質堅重
The liver receives the bile-making or portal vessels.	肝餧紫血生膽之管
Internal lobules are most numerous.	肝小葉至多
The biliary vessels enter these lobules	小葉中多紫血管
The biliary or hepatic duct.	肝之膽汁管
The gall bladder.	膽囊
The cystic duct.	膽囊管
The liver and pancreatic ducts join.	肝膽管與甜肉管相附
And obliquely enter the intestines by one opening.	附而邪入小腸
The spleen is soft and spongy.	脾質鬆軟
Of a purple colour.	脾色深紫
Its surface is round and smooth.	脾稽圓而滑
It varies in size.	脾大小無定

Vessels enter by a transverse fissure	脾橫縫血管所出入
The pancreas resembles the salivary glands.	甜肉畧似生水核
Is behind the stomach, and in front of the spine.	甜肉在胃後脊骨前
It resembles a tongue in shape.	甜肉形似舌
Its pointed extremity touches the spleen.	甜肉尖抵脾
Its head is in contact with the duodenum.	甜肉頭抵小腸曲處

THE DIGESTIVE FUNCTION. 食物消化功用

Food is designed to nourish the body.	食物所以養育身體
It supplies the waste of the blood.	食物補血耗之
Hunger informs us when we should eat	饑則思食以補之
Thirst when we should drink.	渴則思飲以補之
Aliments are divided into nine classes.	食物分九類
Farinaceous aliments.	一穀木之類
Mucilaginous aliments.	二瓜蔬之類
Saccharine aliments.	三甘果糖飴之類
Acidulous aliments.	四酸果之類
Fatty and oily aliments.	五油脂膏之類
Caseous or milk aliments.	六牛乳之類
Gelatinous aliments.	七樹汁魚膠獸膠
Albuminous aliments.	八蛋青之類
Fibrinous aliments.	九禽獸肉類
The successive steps or process of digestion.	消化功用次第
The hand takes and presents the food to the mouth.	手取食物送至口
The jaws separate and the lips receive the food.	牙骨開唇接食物
The teeth masticate it.	牙齒咀嚼食物
Powerful muscles assist this operation.	牙床大肉助咬嚼
Saliva is secreted and mixes with the food.	六核生水勻拌食物

The pressure of the tongue forces it into the gullet.	舌端抵膈偪物入喉
This contracting, passes it over the wind-pipe.	喉歛偪物過氣管口
The epiglottis closely covers its entrance.	會厭遮蓋氣管口
The œsophagus transmits it to the stomach.	食管接物送入胃
The food reaching the stomach is there digested.	物入胃而消化
Three processes assist in digestion.	胃消化三功用互助
First, the peristaltic movements of the stomach.	一運動勻轉令消化
Second, the secretion of gastric juice.	二生津液消化食物
Third, the natural heat of the stomach.	三本熱消化食物
The fluid is first absorbed by minute vessels.	水先吸入微絲管
The rest is digested into chyme.	餘在胃中化爲糜
The pylorus relaxes and it enters the duodenum.	幽門開糜入小腸
Is intermixed with the bile and pancreatic juice.	與膽汁甜肉汁勻合
And after this undergoes many changes.	勻合後糜質全改變
It separates into a fine and coarser part.	此處分別精液渣滓
The finer portion is white like milk.	精液色白如乳
A number of minute vessels absorb it.	衆微管攝吸精液
These vessels are called lacteals.	此管名曰吸液管
They pass through the mesenteric glands.	此小管經腸膜之核
They join and form the thoracic duct.	衆管合爲吸液總管
It ascends in front of the spine.	總液管上脊骨之前
In the neck it communicates with the veins.	至左頸通迴血管
The chyle there enters into the circulation.	津液入運行之血
The refuse is passed through the ileocæcal valve.	渣滓經闌門入大腸

And by the large intestine expelled. 渣滓由大腸傳出

The Thoracic Viscera. 胸背心肺部位

The chest is surrounded by bone and muscle.	胸背內周圍肉骨
Is narrow above and broad below.	胸背內上窄下濶
Its base is the diaphragm.	膈肉爲胸下底
Its upper part is bounded by the first rib.	第一脊骨爲胸上界
Before by the sternum.	胸骨在前
Behind by the spine.	脊骨在後
Its sides by the ribs.	脊骨圍護左右
A septum divides it into two cavities.	肺膜隔分左右
On the right side is the right lung.	隔膜右爲右肺
On the left, the heart and left lung.	隔膜左爲左肺及心
The pericardium or heart purse.	心膜膜
Its reflected portion is attached to the sternum.	心膜膜翻轉連胸骨
The heart is a hollow muscle.	心如肉團有孔竅
Its base is above.	心底在上
Its apex is downwards and to the left side.	心尖向下偏左
The great vessels enter at its base.	總血管出入心底
A middle septum divides the heart into two halves.	心膈肉居中分左右
These united make one entire heart.	左右二體合爲一心
The right and left side do not communicate.	左右心畧不相通
Previous to birth they do communicate.	兒未呼吸左右心相通
The heart has four chambers.	心有四房
The upper are the auricles, the lower the ventricles.	上爲上房下爲下房
The auricles receive the circulating blood.	上房接受運行之血
The ventricles propel it through the body.	下房偪血運行全體

The left ventricle is larger than the right.	左下房大過右下房
The left is the systemic heart, the right the pulmonic.	心左屬全體右屬肺
The left auricles receives the pulmonary veins.	左上房通肺心迴管
The left ventricle the aorta.	左下房通總脈管
The right auricle opens into the venæ cavæ.	右上房通總迴管
The right ventricle into the pulmonary artery.	右下房通心肺總脈管
The auricles are thin, ventricles are thick.	心上房薄下房厚
The auriculo-ventricular opening.	上下房之間有戶
The left has the mitral valve to close it.	左戶兩門扇張翕
The right the tricuspid valve.	右戶三門扇張翕
The mouth of the great vessels is guarded by valves.	總脈管口半月門開合
The semilunar valves of the aorta.	總脈管口半月門三
The semilunar valves of the pulmonary artery.	心肺總脈管口三門
The heart has it own nourishing vessels.	心本體養血管

The lungs fill the sides of the chest	肺體佈滿胸脅
Conical above, broad below.	肺形下闊上銳
The entire base rests on the diaphragm.	肺下界滿抵膈肉
Their outer surface is round & smooth.	肺外面圓滑
They are light and spungy.	肺質輕鬆
Of a reddish and grey colour mixed.	肺淺紅雜白灰色
The pleura or investing membrane.	肺胞膜
Is reflected back and lines the ribs.	肺胞膜翻轉附脊骨
Where it doubles on itself, the air and blood-vessels enter.	翻轉處氣血管所入
These are then divided into innumerable branches.	入後支脈愈分愈多
The right lung has three lobes, the left two.	肺葉右三左二

The internal lobules are minute and beyond number.	肺裏小葉極微而多
Each lobule has air and blood-vessels.	小葉皆有氣管血管
The terminus of the air tubes are the air cells.	氣尾管小胞名氣胞
On these air cells ramify the minute blood-vessels.	氣胞上微管分佈
The smaller air tubes unite, and make larger ones.	衆微管合爲大氣管
Each lung sends out one large air tube.	左右肺各出大氣管
These unite and form the trachea.	兩大氣管合爲總氣管
The cartilaginous rings of the trachea.	總氣管脆骨如圓玦
The epiglottis is its opening and shutting door.	會厭爲總氣管門扇
The larynx or voice organ	總氣管頭音聲所出
The prominent part is called the contracted throat.	外凸者名結喉
Four cartilages form the voice organ.	四脆骨保護出聲處
Within are the vocal cords.	出聲處內有小肉帶
These cords or bands are placed horizontally.	肉帶前後橫牽
Between them is a triangular fissure.	肉帶中間成三角形
Larynx is larger in men than in women	出聲處男大女小
Sound is produced by the air being forcibly expelled.	呼氣偪經此處出聲
The vocal cords are put into vibration.	聲出因肉帶搖動
If tense and shortened, the tone is high.	肉帶緊短則聲高
If the opposite, the tone is deep.	肉帶鬆長則聲低
The cartilages are drawn close in high tones.	脆骨節縮短則聲高
Are separated and relaxed in deep low tones.	脆骨節舒長則聲低
Musical notes depend on the size and length of the tube.	樂聲高低依箭長短
The lips, tongue, mouth and throat, all assist to form speech.	口舌唇喉助出言語
If they are complete there is a clear utterance.	全備則言語明白

If imperfect the speech is indistinct.	不全備不能言語清楚
Animals have sound without speech.	禽獸有聲不能言語
Man only possesses this wonderful faculty.	人言語之機至奧妙

ON THE CIRCULATION OF THE BLOOD. 血運行功用

Food digested is converted into blood.	食物消化爲血
Circulating blood nourishes the whole body.	血運行養育全體
All the secretions are formed from the blood.	各津液皆血所生
In the blood are round particles called globules.	血中有圓物名血輪
These corpuscles are very minute and numerous.	血輪極小而多
The colour of the blood is caused by them.	血色在輪
Three-fourths of the blood is water.	血中水居四分之一
The blood globules form one-seventh.	血輪居七分之一
The rest is flesh fibres, albumen, oil, &c.	餘爲肉絲蛋青油等物
Flesh fibres is called fibrine.	肉絲番名費皮連
Blood at rest separates into two parts.	血出分結不結二種
The coagulum is globules and fibrine united.	結者血輪肉絲相連
The uncoagulated part is called serum.	不結者名爲黃水
Blood is of a scarlet or purple colour.	血有赤紫二色
The arteries convey the red blood.	脈管運行赤血徧體
Veins the purple or black blood.	迴管運行紫血
The capillaries are a net work of vessels.	微絲管如網佈全體
Intermediate between the arteries and veins.	微絲管居脈管迴管間
The blood undergoes many changes in them.	赤血過微絲管多改變
Red blood is changed into black blood.	赤血改變色紫
The veins return it to the heart & lungs.	紫血入迴管歸心肺

The heart is the central organ of the circulation.	心爲運血妙器
By its contractions the blood is forced into the aorta.	心舒縮偪血入總脈管
The aortic branches distribute it.	總脈管支分血佈全體
The power resides in the muscles of the heart.	運行之力在心肉
The heart contracts and dilates unceasingly.	心肉舒縮不息
The heart's propulsion constitutes the pulse.	心偪血作脈
The pulse is quick or low, strong or weak.	脈遲數與心相應
Corresponding to the action of the heart.	脈力大小與心相應
The left side of the heart contains red blood.	左心但有赤血
The right side black blood only.	右心但有紫血
Its orifices & valves aid the circulation.	心門戶助血運行
The circulation is quickest in the arteries.	血在脈管運行至速
Slower in the veins and capillaries.	入微絲管廻管則遲
The valves of the veins aid its upward movement.	廻管門助血上不落
The animal heat is in the blood.	人身本熱在赤血
Respiration is its chief source.	肺呼吸令血熱
Red or arterial blood contains oxygen.	赤血中有養氣
Good blood abounds in red globules.	赤血輪多者血足
It renders the body vigorous and strong.	全體精力倚賴赤血
Poor blood is the cause of debility.	赤血淡者力少
Venous blood contains carbonic acid.	紫血中有炭氣
Is impure and unfit for use.	此血有毒不合用
It returns to the heart and lungs to be purified.	紫血歸心肺改變毒
The carbon is exchanged for oxygen.	肺出炭氣接養氣
Respiration is the function of the lungs.	呼出吸入肺所管理
Its rate corresponds with the heart.	呼吸遲速與心相應

There are four beats to one expiration and inspiration.	一呼一吸心跳四次
These are involuntary and independent functions.	跳與呼吸非人自主
Life depends upon their proper action.	心肺功用生命倚賴

THE URINARY APPARATUS. 生溺生精之器

The kidneys.	內腎
Their inner and outer border.	內腎之內外界
The ureter.	內腎溺管
Its expanded part or pelvis.	溺管之囊
The renal blood-vessels.	內腎血管
The fissure in which they enter.	內界縫管所入
The bladder.	膀胱
Its summit or upper part.	膀胱頂
Its base.	膀胱底
Its neck or prostate.	膀胱蒂
The coats of the bladder.	膀胱皮肉三層
Ureters open into the bladder obliquely.	內腎溺管斜入膀胱
Vesiculæ seminales.	藏精囊在膀胱底
The urethra.	膀胱溺管
The testes.	外腎
The scrotum.	外腎囊
The investing membrane.	外腎胞膜
The spermatic cord.	外腎精管血管
The spermatic vessels enter the urethra.	精管由精囊入溺管

THE SECRETIONS OF THE BODY. 全體津液

e tears.	眼淚
m of the eye.	眼睫津液

s of the nose.	鼻孔津液
of the ear.	耳臘
a.	口水
s of the air passages.	氣管津液
s of the alimentary canal.	食管至大小腸津液
ic juice.	胃津液
ile.	肝膽汁
reatic juice.	甜肉汁
arine.	內腎津液卽溺
emen.	外腎津液卽精
milk.	乳津液卽乳汁
sweat.	皮津液卽汗
s fluid.	各胞膜津液如水
via.	各交節津液如膠

The General Functions. 總論功用

tions of the brain and spinal cord.	腦及腦髓功用
tions of the five senses.	五官功用
nutritive functions.	消化食物養身功用
iratory function.	呼吸功用
ulatory function.	運行血功用
retory function.	生津液功用
retory function.	出無用之津液功用
erative function.	生育子女功用
ction of locomotion.	骨肉運動功用

The Human Soul. 人之靈魂

understanding.	覺悟知識

The faculty of thinking and planning.	思慮計謀
Of judging and choosing.	酌量審擇
Of comparing and deciding.	分別決斷
The memory.	記憶往事
The moral sentiments.	五常之性
Virtuous thoughts or principles.	道念
The passions.	情欲
Good and bad intentions.	志意善惡
The moral sense or conscience.	艮心告語善惡

NAMES OF EXTERNAL PARTS. 外體名稱

Head.	頭
Vertex or crown.	嶺頂
Fontanelle.	顖門
Parietal eminences.	頭角
Frontal eminences.	額角
Occipital eminence.	腦後根
The hair of the head.	頭髮
Its boundary line in front.	髮際
The temples.	太陽穴
Eyebrows.	眉
Root of the nose.	山根
The eyes.	眼
The eyelids.	眼胞
Eyelashes.	眼睫毛
External angle of the eye.	眼外眥
Internal angle.	眼內眥
The face.	臉面
The nose.	鼻

idge of the nose.   梁 鼻準

) of the nose.   鼻

eeks.   腮

ular prominence.   顴

llow of the cheeks.   頤

in.   頦 即 下巴

r.   耳 輪廓

ge lobe of the ear.   耳 垂

all lobe of the ear.   耳 底

or part of the ear.   耳

口

the lip.   唇

part of upper lip.   鬚

ominent part of the throat.   人 中 喉

llow above the sternum.   結 嗌盆

oulders.   缺

ck.   肩

nt part of the chest.   背 膻

atral part of it.   胸 窩頭

ples of the breast.   心 字口 骨

ver border of the ribs.   乳 臂

of the stomach.   人

n.   胃 凹臂

illa   大

ow.   腋

f the arm.   肘

n.   肘

小

手

腕

Outer angle.	手外踝
Inner angle.	手內踝
The back of the hand.	手掌
The palm of the hand.	手心
The fingers.	手指
Space between thumb and finger.	手栱指
The thumb.	大指指
Index finger.	食指
Middle finger.	中指
Nameless or ring finger.	無名指
Little finger.	小指
Finger nails.	指甲
The markings of the fingers.	指螺紋
The loins.	腰
The abdomen.	肚腹
The navel.	臍
Lower part of the abdomen.	小腹
The buttocks.	臀
The hips.	胯
The thigh.	大腿
The knee-pan.	膝蓋
The bend of the knee.	膝凹
The leg.	小腿
The calf of the leg.	腿囊
The outer ankle.	足外踝
The inner ankle.	足內踝
Space above the heel.	足脛
The heel.	足後跟
The instep.	足掌心
The sole of the foot.	足心

TERMS USED IN MEDICINE. 內部病證名目

Ague.	瘧症即寒熱往來
Anæmia—bloodlessness.	血虛薄皮色白
Anasarca—general dropsy.	全體皮膜水腫
Aphonia—loss of voice.	失音
,, Dumbness.	喉瘂
Apthæ—white specks of the mouth.	口唇生白泡
Apoplexy from effusion of blood.	腦血中風
,, Serous apoplexy.	腦水中風
Ascites—abdominal dropsy.	腹脹
Asphyxia.	人不吸生氣死
Asthma.	氣喘
,, Humoural asthma.	痰喘
Atrophy of the muscles.	肌肉瘦
Biliary disorders.	膽之病
,, Bile diminished.	膽汁太少
,, Bile excessive.	膽汁太多
,, Bile vitiated.	膽汁變質
,, Calculi.	膽淋
Bladder, diseases of,	膀胱病
,, Inflamed.	膀胱炎
,, Irritable.	膀胱不安
Blood, diseases of,	血之病
,, Congestion of,	血積聚一處
,, Excess of,	血太多
,, Deficiency of,	血太少
,, Poor and thin,	血輪少稀薄

E

Brain, inflammation of,	腦體生炎
„ Softening of,	腦質變軟
„ Abscess of,	腦體生膿
„ Inflammation of the membranes.	腦胞內外生炎
„ Dropsy of,	腦胞水漲
Bronchitis, acute and chronic.	氣瞀新舊災
Bronchocele.	結喉之下核變大
Cachexy or bad habit of body.	身虛血毒
Cancer, internal,	內部癩疽
„ of the stomach.	胃癩疽
Catarrh or common cold.	傷風
Chicken-pox—varicella.	水痘
Cholera.	霍亂吐瀉
Colic.	肚腹暴痛反覆
Congestion of the brain and lungs.	血積聚腦肺
„ of the liver and spleen.	血積聚肝脾
Constipation.	大便秘結
Consumption, pulmonary,	肺勞症
Cough.	欬嗽
„ Without expectoration.	乾欬
„ With expectoration.	痰欬
„ Spitting of blood.	欬血
Cow-pox.	種痘瘄粒
Dandriff.	髮根風癬皮
Debility, general,	身虛弱
Delirum tremens.	中酒累腦
Diabetes.	溺太多味變甜
Diarrhœa.	瀉泄
Digestive organs, diseases of,	消化之器病証
Diseases divided into acute & chronic.	病分新舊

Diseases, Active and passive,		病分虛實
"	Organic or structural,	臟腑本體之病
"	Functional,	臟腑功用之病
"	Idiopathic,	臟腑本體自病
"	Symptomatic,	別部延累之病
"	Contagious,	傳染病證
"	Hereditary,	父母延累病症
"	Congenital,	嬰兒出世之病
"	Endemic,	地土所生之病
"	Epidemic,	傳染時行之病
"	Pestilential,	温疫病
"	Diagnosis of,	醫者審察病証
"	Prognosis of,	分別輕重可治否
"	Treatment of,	用法療治
Dysentery.		紅白痢
Dyspepsia.		不消化
Dyspnœa or quick breathing.		喘促
Epileptic convulsions.		癇症俗名發羊瘹
Exhaustion.		精力耗盡
Face, paralysis of,		口眼歪斜
Fainting or syncope.		失魂
Fatuity—dementia.		發狂變獃
Fever.		熱病
"	Ephemeral,	暫時發熱
"	Continued,	發熱不止
"	Complicated,	發熱累內部
"	Typhus,	發熱身虛弱
"	Putrid,	發熱血有毒
"	Yellow,	發熱黃証
"	With petechiæ,	熱証發癍

Fever, Remittent,	發熱時輕時重	
„ Intermittent,	寒熱往來又名瘧	
„ Quotidian,	瘧一日一作	
„ Tertian,	瘧間日一作	
„ Quartan,	瘧間二日一作	
Flatulence.	肚腹內有風氣	
Gastralgia—pain of the stomach.	胃痛不消化	
Gastritis—inflammation of the stomach.	胃炎	
Giddiness—vertigo.	頭昏暈	
Gout.	酒脚病	
Gravel.	沙淋	
Hæmorrhage or internal bleeding.	內部血出	
„ From the nose.	鼻血	
„ From the gums.	牙齦血出	
„ From the lungs.	肺血欬出	
„ From the stomach.	胃血吐出	
„ From the bowels.	大小腸血瀉出	
„ From the urinary organs.	內腎膀胱血溺出	
„ From the womb.	子宮血出	
Hæmorrhoids or piles.	痔瘡	
Headache.	頭痛	
Heart diseases.	心之病	
„ Sudden pain of,	心暴痛	
„ Palpitation of,	心跳	
„ Inflammation of,	心炎	
„ Enlargement of,	心體變大	
„ Rupture of,	心房裂	
„ Diseases of the valves,	心房門病	
„ Inflammation of the membranes,	心胞炎	
„ Dropsy of,	心胞有水	

„	Diseases of similunar valves.	總脊三半月門病
„	Auscultory signs of.	聞聲辨証
Hiccup.		呃逆
Hydrophobia—canine madness.		狂犬咬令人癲
Inflammation of the viscera.		臟腑炎又名炎法美順
„	of the brain.	腦炎
„	of the lungs.	肺炎
„	of the tongue.	舌炎
„	of the salivary glands.	生水核炎
„	of the throat.	喉炎
„	of the stomach.	胃炎
„	of the intestines.	大小腸炎
„	of the liver.	肝炎
„	of the kidneys.	內腎炎
„	of the bladder.	膀胱炎
„	of the uterus.	子宮炎
„	of the investing membranes	各臟腑胞膜炎
Influenza.		時行傷風傳染
Inoculation.		種苗痘
Insanity, kinds of,		癲狂妄有別
„	Dementia.	糊塗爲癲
„	Mania.	猛力爲狂
„	Mental aberration.	妄言妄想爲妄
Jaundice.		疸黃病
Kidney, diseases of,		內腎病
„	Functional disorder.	內腎功用病
„	Structural diseases.	內腎本體變壞
„	Atrophy of,	內腎本體變小
„	Calculous diseases of,	內腎沙石淋
Laryngitis or inflammation of larynx.		氣管出聲處生炎

,,	Croup of children.	嬰兒出聲處生炎
Leprosy.		痲瘋
Liver, diseases of,		肝病
,,	Functional disorder of,	肝功用病
,,	Abscess of,	肝生膿瘡
,,	Enlargement and induration of,	肝質變堅變大
Locket-jaw—tetanus.		牙關緊閉
Lungs, diseases of,		肺病
,,	Structural disease of,	肺本體病
,,	Functional disease of,	肺功用病
Malaria.		腐毒之氣
Marsh fever.		霑濕之地生病
Measles.		痲症
Mesenteric glands, diseased.		腸胘膜之核生病
Mortification, internal.		內部死肉症
Neuralgia or nerve pain.		腦氣筋痛
,,	of the face.	面腦筋痛
,,	of the heart.	心腦筋痛
,,	of the stomach.	胃腦筋痛
Obstruction of the bowels.		大便之路不通
Œsophagus, diseases of,		食物管病
,,	Stricture of,	食管變窄
Ovarian dropsy.		子宮核水腹
Pancreas, diseases of.		甜肉經病
Paralysis.		癱瘓
,,	of motion.	運動功用癱
,,	sensation.	知覺功用癱
,,	of both united.	運動知覺全癱
,,	of one side.	左右截癱
,,	of half the body.	上下截癱

Pericarditis, acute and chronic.	心胞新舊炎
Peritonitis, acute and chronic.	肚腹胞膜新舊炎
Pleurisy, acute and chronic.	肺胞膜新舊炎
Pneumonia.	肺本體炎
Prostate glands, diseases of,	膀胱蒂病
Psoriasis, various kinds of,	各種癬
Pustules of the skin.	皮生膿胞
Quinsy—cynanche tonsillaris.	喉左右核生炎
Red rash.	周身皮生紅點
Rheumatism acute and chronic.	風濕新舊症
Ringworm.	禿瘡
Scabies or itch.	疥瘡乾濕二種
Scaly diseases of the skin.	皮生鱗之病
Sciatica.	臀下腦氣筋痛
Scrofulous enlargements.	瘰癧
Scurvy.	身虛牙肉脚瘡泄血
Secretions, diseases of,	津液之病
Sick or bilious headache.	頭痛欲嘔
Skin diseases.	皮病
Small-pox—variola.	出痘
„ Modified and confluent.	痘毒分輕重
Sore throat, ulcerated,	喉爛
Spinal cord, inflammation of,	腦髓炎
„ Dropsy of,	腦髓水
„ Irritation of,	腦髓不安
„ Softening of,	腦髓變壞
Spleen, diseases of,	脾病
„ Congestion of,	脾接血太多
„ Inflammation of,	脾炎
„ Enlargement of,	脾變大

Spleen, induration or softening of.	脾質變堅變軟
Stomach, diseases of,	胃病
„ Functional disorder of,	胃功用病
„ Inflammation of,	胃炎
„ Ulceration of lining membrane.	胃內皮爛
„ Cancer of,	胃癰
„ Perforation of,	胃壞穿穴
„ Irritation of,	胃腦筋不安
Stricture of the bowels.	大小腸變窄
„ Do. of the rectum.	直腸變窄
„ Temporary or permanent.	窄分久暫
Syphilitic blotches.	疔毒之瘢
Tenesmus.	痢症裏急
Tongue, diseases of,	舌病
Tubercle of the lungs.	肺體都比週力
Ulceration of the bowels.	大小腸潰爛
Urinary organs, diseases of,	生溺器之病
Urine, excess of,	溺太多
„ Suppression of,	溺不生
„ Morbid alterations of,	溺變質
„ Incontinence of,	遺溺
Vaccination.	種牛痘
Vomiting.	嘔吐
Wind-pipe, diseases of,	大氣管病
Worms, intestinal,	蛔蟲
„ Tape worm.	扁蟲
„ Round worm.	圓蟲
„ Thread worm.	小蟲

TERMS USED IN SURGERY. 外科名目

Abdomen, wounds and injuries of,		肚腹外傷
Abscess.		膿瘡
„	Recent or acute.	新膿瘡
„	Old or chronic.	舊膿瘡
„	Large and small.	大小膿瘡
„	Of the orbit.	眼窠膿瘡
„	Of bone.	骨膿瘡
„	Of the brain.	腦膿瘡
„	Of the joints.	交節膿瘡
„	Of the loins.	腰膿瘡
Aneurism.		脈管跳血囊
„	Of the arch of the aorta.	總脈管栱跳血囊
„	At the bend of the elbow.	肘凹跳血囊
„	Popliteal aneurism.	膝凹跳血囊
„	Rupture of,	血囊自裂
„	Spontaneous cure of,	血囊自止
Antrum, diseases of,		上牙床骨穴之病
Anus, diseases of,		直腸肛門之病
„	Imperforate anus.	小兒初生無肛門
„	Fistula of,	肛門瘻管
„	Inflamed piles.	內外痔炎痛
„	Bleeding piles.	外痔標血
„	Abscess in perineum.	肛門前生膿瘡
„	Prolapsus of the bowel.	脫肛
„	Undue contraction of sphincter.	肛門緊縮
„	Stricture of the rectum.	直腸變窄
„	Cancer of rectum.	直腸癰

F

Bladder, diseases of,		膀胱之病
,,	Irritable bladder.	膀胱不安
,,	Chronic inflammation of,	膀胱內皮舊炎
,,	Paralysis of,	膀胱癱瘓
,,	Calculus of,	膀胱石淋
,,	Abscess of the prostate,	膀胱蒂膿瘡
,,	Enlargement of prostate,	膀胱蒂變大
,,	Calculus imbedded in,	膀胱蒂石淋
Boils, large and small,		大小暑瘤
Bones, diseases of,		骨病
,,	Inflamed bone.	骨炎
,,	Inflamed periosteum.	骨衣炎
,,	Exostosis or bony tumor.	骨瘤
,,	Rickets.	軟曲骨
,,	Caries.	爛骨
,,	Necrosis.	死骨
Brain, injuries of,		腦外傷
,,	Contusion of the head	頭跌打傷
,,	Wounds of the head.	頭刀刃傷
,,	Compression of the brain.	頭骨斷壓腦
,,	Inflam: of brain and membranes.	腦胞炎
,,	Concussion of the brain.	腦體震撞
,,	Protrusion of the brain.	頭骨斷裂腦出
,,	Suppuration and softening.	腦生膿質變軟
Breast, diseases of,		乳病
,,	General enlargement.	乳體生大
,,	Lacteal swelling.	乳管生大
,,	Inflammation acute and chronic.	乳炎分新舊
,,	Milk abscess.	乳膿瘡
,,	Neuralgia of the breast.	乳腦筋痛

Breast, Tumours of the breast.	乳生肉瘤	
„	Cancer of the breast.	乳癰
„	Disease of the nipple.	乳頭爛
„	Retraction of the nipple.	乳頭縮
Burns.	火燒傷	
Cancer, hard and soft.	癰疽堅軟二種	
„	ulcerated.	癰疽潰爛
„	of bone.	骨癰
„	of the eye.	眼癰
„	of the lip.	唇癰
„	of the nose.	鼻癰
„	of the scrotum.	腎囊癰
„	of the tongue.	舌癰
Carbuncle.	毒膿瘡又名發背	
Chest, wounds and injuries of,	胸部外傷	
Chilblains.	凍瘡	
Deformities of the body.	肢體不正	
„	Undue prominence of forehead.	凸額
„	Undue size of the head.	大頭
„	Nose bent on one side.	歪鼻
„	Strabismus or squinting.	邪眼
„	Divided or hare lip.	缺唇
„	Wry neck.	歪頭
„	Chicken breast.	雞胸
„	Curvature of spine, angular.	駝背
„	Lateral curvature.	曲背
„	Deformities of hands and feet.	手足跛蹴
Dislocation.	骨交節脫	
„	of lower jaw.	下牙床骨交節脫
„	of the collar bone.	鎖柱骨脫

Dislocation of the shoulder.		肩臂骨交節脫
„	of the elbow.	肘交節脫
„	of the wrist.	手腕交節脫
„	of the finger joints.	指骨交節脫
„	of the thigh.	大腿骨髀白脫
„	of the ankle.	腿足交節脫
„	of the knee-pan.	膝蓋脫
Diseases of the ear.		耳之病
„	Foreign body in the ear.	外物塞耳竅
„	Undue secretion of wax.	耳膿太多
„	Inflammation of auditory canal.	耳外竅生炎
„	Otorrhœa or discharge.	耳外竅流膿
„	Small tumours of the ear.	耳外竅生瘤
„	Disease of the tympanum.	耳膜爛壞
„	Inflammation of the internal ear.	耳中竅炎
„	Acute pain of the ear.	耳內痛劇
„	Function impaired.	耳功用病不聰
„	Entire deafness.	耳器壞全聾
Diseases of the eye.		眼之病
„	Inflammation acute and chronic.	眼炎新舊
„	Wounds of the eye.	眼外傷
„	Foreign bodies in the eye.	外物入眼
„	Diseases of the eyelids.	眼蓋病
„	Hordeolum or stye.	眼睫小膿瘡
„	Opthalmia tarsi.	眼蓋內皮生炎
„	Trichiasis--turning in of eyelashes.	睫毛倒插
„	Entropium—turning in of eyelid.	眼蓋向內翻轉
„	Ectropium—eversion of eyelid.	眼蓋向外翻轉
„	Ptosis---inability to raise the lid.	眼上胞墜下
„	Small tumours of the eyelids.	眼蓋生小肉瘤

,,	Granular lids.	眼蓋內皮不平
,,	Diseases of lacrymal sac.	眼囊炎有膿
,,	Closure of ducts.	淚管塞
,,	Secretion deficient.	淚少眼乾
,,	Secretion too abundant.	淚太多
,,	Obstruction of nasal canal.	入鼻淚管塞
,,	Diseases of the eyeball.	眼球之病
,,	Inflammation of the conjunctiva	罩睛皮新舊炎
,,	Catarrhal opthalmia.	淚炎
,,	Scrofulous opthalmia.	盧炎畏光
,,	Purulent opthalmia.	膿炎
,,	Pterygium—fleshy growth.	努肉扳睛
,,	Inflammation of the cornea.	明角罩炎
,,	Opacity of the cornea.	明角罩昏
,,	Albugo or specks.	明角罩生點
,,	Leucoma.	明角罩生瞖
,,	Conical cornea.	明角罩一邊尖凸
,,	Staphyloma.	明角罩全凸
,,	Ulceration of the cornea.	明角罩潰爛
,,	Inflammation of sclerotic coat.	眼白殼生炎
,,	Inflammation of the iris.	眼簾生炎
,,	Prolapsus of the iris.	眼簾流出
,,	Closure of the pupil.	瞳人塞
,,	Cataract.	睛珠變質不明
,,	Glaucoma.	大房水變質
,,	Amaurosis.	發青光
,,	Abscess of the eyeball.	眼球生膿瘡
,,	Dropsy of the eyeball.	眼球水脹
,,	Impaired vision.	視物不明
,,	Total blindness.	眼全壞不能視

Fracture of bone.	折斷骨
,, Simple fracture.	骨折斷皮肉未傷
,, Compound fracture.	骨折斷累皮肉
,, Fracture with dislocation.	骨折斷又脫
,, Fracture of the skull.	頭骨折斷
,, The nasal bones.	鼻梁骨折斷
,, The vertebræ.	脊背骨折斷
,, The ribs.	脅骨折斷
,, The collar bone.	鎖柱骨折斷
,, The scapula.	飯匙骨折斷
,, Bones of the leg and arm.	四肢骨折斷
,, Double fracture.	一骨兩處折斷
,, Comminuted fracture.	骨折斷碎爛
,, Transverse fracture.	骨橫折
,, Oblique fracture.	骨斜折
,, Broken but not displaced,	骨拆未離
Gangrene, dry and humid.	死肉乾濕二種
,, from want of blood.	死肉因血不至
,, from the effect of cold.	死肉因凍㾼
,, from external injuries.	死肉因外傷
,, from long pressure.	死肉因壓著
Glands, enlargement of,	諸核變大
Gonorrhœa.	流白濁
Hæmorrhage, external,	外傷血流
,, from a wounded artery.	脈管傷流血不止
,, from injured kidneys.	內腎傷流血
,, from injured urethra.	溺管傷流血
,, from injured rectum.	直腸傷流血
,, from external cuts.	皮破流血
,, from extraction of teeth.	脫牙流血

,,	from leech bites.	蟣吮後血不止
Hernia or protusion of the bowels.		小腸氣卽小腸疝
,,	Oblique or scrotal hernia.	小腸邪墜入腎囊
,,	Direct or femoral hernia.	小腸直墜入大腿
,,	Umbilical hernia.	小腸墜至臍
Hydrocele.		腎囊水疝
Joints, diseases of,		交節之病
,,	Inflam. of synovial membrane	交節胞膜生炎
,,	Ulceration of the cartilages.	交節骨髓筋帶壞
,,	Anchylosis.	交節相連不動
,,	Disease of the hip joint.	脾白之病
Mouth, diseases of,		口之病
,,	Swollen tongue.	舌腫大
,,	Ulceration of the tongue.	舌爛
,,	Tongue tied.	舌筋帶短
,,	Ranula or salivary tumor.	舌底水核管變大
,,	Elongation of uvula.	吊鐘長
,,	Enlargement of the tonsils.	喉左右核變大
,,	Scurvy of the gums.	牙肉腫流血
,,	Gum boil.	牙肉生小膿瘡
,,	Epulis or tumor of the gums.	牙肉生瘤
,,	Cleft palate.	上腭通鼻之縫
Nose, affections of,		鼻之病
,,	Epistaxis or hæmorrhage from,	鼻血
,,	Nasal polypus.	鼻蛇
,,	Imperforate nostrils.	鼻孔塞
,,	Syphilitic ulceration of,	鼻孔生疔瘡
Rheumation of the joints.		交節風濕
Salivation.		六核生水太多
Scabbing.		瘡痂

Wounds from bites of animals.	獸類咬傷
„ Superficial and deep wounds.	外傷分輕重淺深
„ Of the joints.	交節外傷
„ Of the scalp.	頭皮肉外傷
„ Of the neck.	頸皮肉外傷
„ Of the bowels and gall-bladder.	腸及膽囊外傷
„ Of the stomach and liver.	肝胃外傷
„ Of the heart and lungs.	心肺外傷

SURGICAL INSTRUMENTS. 外科各器

Abscess lancet.	放膿刀
Amputation knife.	劏手足大刀
Aneurism needle.	血囊穿線鈍針
Artery forceps.	脈管鉗
Bandages of various kinds.	各種布帶
Bistoury, sharp pointed,	銳彎刀
„ blunt pointed,	鈍彎刀
„ straight,	銳直刀
Bone cutting forceps.	剪骨直鉗
„ curved forceps.	剪骨曲鉗
„ nippers.	柑骨鉗
„ elevator.	撬骨器
Bleeding lancet.	放血刀
Bullet forceps.	彈丸鉗
„ scoop.	彈丸挖
Bougies.	通溺管器
Catheter, silver,	引溺銀管
Caustic holder.	裝各息的柄
ry.	烙炙器
	半管引導針

Dissecting forceps.	便用鑷
Dressing forceps.	便用鉗
Ear speculum.	照耳器
Exploring needle.	探膿水針
Exploring sound.	探石淋器
Eye instruments.	眼科各器
„ Cataract knife.	取睛珠刀
„ Couching needle, curved.	撥睛珠彎針
„ Couching needle, straight.	撥睛珠直針
„ Entropium forceps.	柑眼胞皮瀾鑷
„ Iris hook.	彎眼鈎
„ Iris knife.	割眼簾刀
„ Forceps for extracting eyelashes.	拔睫毛鑷
„ Probe.	鍉眼針
„ Scissars, straight and curved.	眼曲直交剪
„ Speculum.	開眼器
„ Syringe.	眼水節
Fracture apparatus.	接骨之器
„ Iron fracture bed.	鐵架
„ Long and short splints.	長短木夾
„ Arm splints.	臂夾
„ Leg splints.	腿夾
Gum lancet.	牙肉刀
Instrument case.	外科藏器篋
„ Leather pocket case.	藏器便用皮包
Lithotomy instruments.	割石淋器
„ Lithotomy knife.	膀胱石淋刀
„ Grooved sound.	引刀器
„ Stone forceps.	石淋鉗
„ Urethral forceps.	溺管石淋鉗

Lithotrity instruments.	夾碎石淋器
Needles, straight and curved.	縫皮彎直針
Polypus forceps.	鼻蛇鉗
Pulley for reducing dislocation.	收束牌白轆轤
Saw, large and small.	大小骨鋸
Scalpel.	小割刀
Scissars of different sizes.	大小交剪
Silver probe.	銀探針
Spring forceps.	踐機鑷
Stethoscope.	問病筩
Stomach pump.	入胃銅水節
Tenaculum or hook.	大小銳鈎
Tourniquet.	止血器機
Tooth forceps, straight and curved.	曲直牙鉗
Trephine or round saw.	頭骨圓鋸
Trocar, large and small.	大小套管針

SURGICAL OPERATIONS. 醫治外証手法

Abstraction of blood.		放血之法
„	Bleeding from the arm.	剌迴管法
„	Cupping.	抽氣放血法
„	Leeching.	放蟥吮血法
„	Puncturing.	小銳刀剌皮法
Acupuncture.		針法
Actual cautery.		烙炙法
Amputation.		割鋸四肢法
„	Flap operation.	兩邊對割法
„	Circular operation.	周圍旋割法
Anæsthesia.		迷蒙忘痛法

53

Bandaging.	綁紮布帶法
Clearing nasal ducts.	通淚管法
Closing wound by plaster.	用膏藥合口法
Closing wound by suture.	用線縫結法
Counter-irritation.	引病外出法
„ Blistering &c.	斑蝥等藥釣膿
„ Issues.	割皮入豆釣膿
„ Seton.	用線穿皮釣膿
„ Escharotics.	用藥爛皮釣膿
„ Moxa.	艾炙法
„ Reddening the skin &c.	鑷皮引血法
Electrifying.	用電器治病法
Elevating depressed bone.	用器舉撬頭骨法
Excision of joints.	割交節法
„ of tumours.	割大小瘤法
„ of diseased testis.	外腎癰毒割法
Extraction of bullets.	拑取彈丸法
„ of teeth.	脫牙法
Healing contused wounds.	醫跌打潰爛法
Lithotomy.	割膀胱石淋法
Ligature of arteries.	綁紮脈管法
Operation for cataract-extraction.	割取睛珠法
„ needle operation-couching.	撥下睛珠法
„ for entropium.	醫治倒睫法
„ for false pupil.	作假瞳人法
„ for hare lip.	縫結缺唇法
„ for cancer.	割癰瘤法
„ for strangulated hernia.	小腸緊結割送法
„ for aneurism.	醫脈管跳血囊法
„ for hydrocele.	引腎囊水外出法

Opening abscess.	放膿法
Passing the catheter.	引溺出法
Reduction of fractures.	接續斷骨法
,, of dislocations.	舒送脫骨法
Removing calculi from urethra.	柑取溺管石淋法
,, foreign bodies from the ear.	柑挖耳孔外物法
,, nasal polypus.	柑取鼻蛇法
,, splinters &c. from the flesh.	外物入肉取出法
Removal of pterygium.	劙努肉扱睛法
,, of staphyloma.	劙凸眼法
Rescuing persons in imminent peril.	急救各法
,, from hanging.	救縊死法
,, from drowning.	救溺死法
,, in syncope.	救頭昏失魂法
,, in convulsion.	救癇病法
,, from effects of cold.	救凍死法
,, from effects of hunger.	救餓死法
,, from suicide.	救自刎法
,, from asphyxia.	救中炭氣昏蒙法
,, from choking.	救吞物塞氣管法
,, from arterial hæmorrhage.	救血標流法
,, from burns and scalds.	救火傷法
,, from poisoning.	救鴉片信石毒法
Stopping hæmorrhage.	止血之法
Snipping the frænum of the tongue.	剪舌底筋帶法
Syringing the ears.	水節洗耳法
Tapping water in the brain.	頭腦放水法
Tapping the chest.	胸部放水法
Tapping the abdomen.	肚腹放水法
Taxis—reduction of hernia.	小腸疝送還法

plication.	用鋼夾醫疝法
.omy.	氣管塞割救法
ng.	圓鋸解頭骨法
cut surfaces.	連合割口法
.ion.	種牛痘法

———◇———

ERMS USED IN MIDWIFERY. 婦科名目

.le pelvis.	婦人尻骨盤
ubis.	橫交骨
physis pubis.	交骨縫
.um.	尾骶骨
.yx.	尾閭骨
. of the pelvis.	骨盤上口
.et of the pelvis.	骨盤下口
.ty of the pelvis.	骨盤之內
.ro-posterior diameter.	骨盤直徑
.sverse diameter.	骨盤橫徑
.que diameter.	骨盤邪徑
.ormed pelvis.	正骨盤
.ed pelvis.	歪骨盤
.ents of the pelvis.	骨盤內容諸腑
bladder in front.	膀胱在前
.ehind.	直腸在後
.termediate.	子宮在中
. the uterus.	子宮之口
.he uterus.	子宮之頸
. the uterus.	云角房
. into fallopian tubes.	通子管之路

Retraction of the tongue.	舌縮塞喉
Abnormal formation of the head.	初生頭不正
Elongation of the head.	初生頭長不圓
Protuberance of scalp.	頭皮有水高凸
Swollen features.	面腫黑
Distorted face.	口角上掛
Retention of urine.	無小便
Retention of meconium.	無黑尿
Swelling of the breasts.	小兒乳旁生炎
Discharge from the eyes.	眼膿炎
Eyes gummed up.	眼眵粘塞
Bleeding from the navel.	臍流血
Navel chafed and ulcerated.	臍紅爛
Irritation of the skin from dirt.	汚濁損皮
Sores of the corners of the mouth.	口脣生瘡
Sores of the ears.	耳輪破爛
Tongue tied.	舌筋短
Convulsions.	痫証
Cold and cough.	傷風欬嗽
Diarrhœa.	腹痛瀉泄
Psoriasis of the scalp.	頭皮生癬
Teething, diseases of,	生牙換牙之病
Measles.	麻証
Small-pox.	痘証
Chicken-pox.	水痘

NAMES OF MEDICINES. 藥品名目

Acid, Acetic,	濃酸醋
„ Citric,	榜檬汁
„ Muriatic,	鹽强水
„ Nitric,	硝强水
„ Nitric diluted.	淡硝强水
„ Sulphuric,	磺强水
„ Sulphuric diluted,	淡磺强水
„ Tartaric,	酸葡萄汁
Alcohol.	極濃酒
Almonds, bitter and sweet,	杏仁甜苦二種
Aloes.	啞囉
Alum.	白礬
„ Dried alum.	枯礬
Amber.	琥珀
Ammonia.	阿摩呢阿
Aniseed.	八角
Artemisia.	艾葉
Armenian bole.	赤石脂
Arrow root.	藕蓮粉
Arsenic, red and white,	紅白信石卽砒霜
Assafœtida.	阿魏
Asses' glue.	阿膠
Barley.	大麥
„ Prepared barley.	薏苡仁
Belladonna.	啤啦吲嘲
Borax.	硼砂
Bezoar.	牛黃

Calomel.	迦路米卽洋輕粉
Camphor.	樟腦
Cassia root.	肉桂
Cantharides.	斑蝥
Capsicum.	辣椒
Caraway.	大茴香
Cardamom.	白豆蔻油
Castor oil.	蓖麻油
Catechu.	兒茶
Caustic—lunar caustic.	各息的
Chalk.	石粉
Chamomile.	野菊花
Charcoal.	炭
China root.	土茯苓
Chives.	薤
Cinchona, red and yellow.	金雞哪黃紅二種
Cinnamon.	桂皮
Cinnabar.	硃砂
Cloves.	丁香
Congee.	粥米
Copper, preparations of,	銅之劑
„ Sulphate of copper.	膽礬
„ Acetate of copper.	銅綠
Cotton.	綿花
Creasote.	幾啊嚧油
Croton-oil.	巴豆油
Cubebs.	澄茄
Cuttle fish bone,	海螵蛸
Distilled water.	蒸水
Decoction of barley,	大麥煮水

Decoction of Cinchona.	金雞哪煮水	
„ Ergot.	耳臥達煮水	
„ Galls.	沒石子煮水	
„ Logwood.	蘇木煮水	
„ Linseed.	胡麻子煮水	
„ Pomegranate.	石榴煮水	
„ Poppy.	罌粟殼煮水	
„ Sarsaparilla.	土茯苓煮水	
„ Starch.	麥漿煮水	
Dovers powder.	叱啤嘮鴉片散	
Ergot.	耳臥達	
Extract of Aloes.	啞囉膏	
„ Belladonna.	啤啦吐嚟膏	
„ Colocynth.	喎囉嘯膏	
„ Gentian.	黃連膏	
„ Opium.	鴉片膏	
„ Rhubarb.	大黃膏	
„ Thorn apple.	醉仙桃膏	
Galls.	沒石子	
Gamboge.	藤黃	
Garlic.	大蒜	
Gentian.	黃連	
Ginger.	生薑	
„ Dried ginger.	乾薑	
Ginseng.	人參	
„ Foreign ginseng.	洋人參	
Grapes.	葡萄子	
Grey powder.	灰色散卽水銀散	
Gum.	水膠	
Hartshorn.	鹿角片	

Hellebore.		蘆薈
Honey.		蜜
Indigo.		靛
Infusion of Aniseed.		八角冲水
"	Catechu.	兒茶冲水
"	Chamomile.	野菊花冲水
"	Coffee.	迦啡冲水
"	Cloves.	丁香冲水
"	Ginger.	生薑冲水
"	Ginseng.	人參冲水
"	Gentian.	黃連冲水
"	Mint.	薄荷冲水
"	Orange-peel.	橙皮冲水
"	Quassia.	白木喇嘜冲水
"	Rhubarb.	大黃冲水
"	Tea.	茶葉冲水
Iodine.		挨阿顛
Ipecac.		叺啤咯
Iron, preparations of,		鐵之劑
"	Iron dust or filings.	鐵末
"	Iron rust.	鐵鏽
"	Red oxide of iron.	鐵紅散
"	Sulphate of iron.	青礬
Isinglass.		魚膠
Jalap.		渣臘
Lard.		猪油
Lead, preparations of,		鉛之劑
"	Acetate or sugar of lead.	鉛散
"	Carbonate or white lead.	鉛粉
"	Litharge.	蜜佗僧

Lead, red lead or minium.	紅丹
Lime.	石灰
Linseed.	胡麻子
Liquorice root.	甘草
Logwood.	蘇木
Long pepper.	蓽撥
Magnesia.	嚜呢沙
Mercurial preparations.	水銀之劑
,, Grey oxide of mercury.	水銀散
,, Red oxide of mercury.	三仙丹
Mixture of camphor.	樟腦水
,, Chalk.	石粉水
Morphia.	嗼啡啞
Musk.	麝香
Mustard.	芥末
Myrrh.	沒藥
Nutmeg.	肉豆蔲
Nux vomica.	馬前
Oils.	油之類
Oil of amber.	琥珀油
,, Aniseed,	八角油
,, Beans,	豆油
,, Cloves,	丁香油
,, Cinnamon,	桂皮油
,, Croton,	巴豆油
,, Linseed,	胡麻子油
,, Peppermint,	薄荷油
,, Nut—ground-nut,	花生油
,, Olive,	橄欖油
,, Turpentine,	松漆油

Olibanum.		乳香
Opium.		鴉片
Orpiment.		雄黃
Pills of aloes.		啞囉丸
,,	Aloes and iron.	啞囉青礬丸
,,	Aloes and myrrh.	啞囉沒藥丸
,,	Aloes and rhubarb.	啞囉大黃丸
,,	Calomel and opium.	迦路米鴉片丸
,,	Colocynth.	喎囉嘶丸
,,	Croton-oil.	巴豆丸
,,	Gentian and rhubarb.	黃連大黃丸
,,	Iron and myrrh.	青礬沒藥丸
,,	Mercury or blue pill.	水銀丸又名藍丸
,,	Opium.	鴉片丸
,,	Opium and lead.	鴉片鉛散丸
,,	Rhubarb.	大黃丸
,,	Rhubarb and ginger.	大黃乾薑丸
,,	Rhubarb and iron.	大黃青礬丸
Plaster of cantharides.		斑蝥硬膏
,,	Isinglass, adhesive plaster.	魚膠合口硬膏藥
,,	Lead, adhesive plaster.	蜜佗僧合口硬膏藥
,,	Resin.	松香硬膏藥
Pepper, black and white,		黑白椒
Pomegranate.		石榴殼
Potash.		䶅
Powder of compound catechu.		兒茶桂皮散
,,	Chalk and cinnamon.	石粉桂皮散
,,	Aromatic powder.	香物糖卽桂皮糖
,,	Cinnamon, nutmeg, ginger.	桂皮白豆蔻散
,,	Ipecac and opium.	叱哖嗒鴉片散

owder of rhubarb and ginger.	大黃薑末散
uassia, or white wood.	白木喇唦
uinine, or ke-na.	雞哪又名桂哪
ain water.	雨水
aisins.	乾葡萄
esin.	松香
hubarb.	大黃
ago.	西穀米
alt-petre—nitrate of potash.	朴硝
oda.	蘇咃
„ Sulphate of soda—salts.	元明粉
tarch.	麥漿
tramonium or thorn apple.	醉仙桃
uet.	脂膏
ugar.	白糖
ulphur.	硫黃末
olution of Alum.	白礬水
„ Arsenic and potash.	信石水
„ Copper.	膽礬水
„ Sugar of lead.	鉛水
„ Lime.	石灰水
„ Caustic.	各息的水
„ Sulphate of zinc.	精鎬水
inctures.	浸酒之類
incture of Ammonia.	阿摩呢阿酒
„ Camphor.	樟腦酒
„ Camphor and opium.	樟腦鴉片酒
„ Cantharides.	斑蝥酒
„ Capsicum.	辣椒酒
„ Catechu.	兒茶酒

I

Tincture of Cinnamon.		桂皮酒
„	Ergot.	耳臥達酒
„	Gentian.	黃連酒
„	Ginger.	生薑酒
„	Iodine.	挨阿顚酒
„	Steel or iron.	鐵酒
„	Myrrh.	沒藥酒
„	Opium.	鴉片酒
„	Opium with cloves &c.	鴉片丁香酒
„	Orange-peel.	橙皮酒
„	Rhubarb.	大黃酒
Ointment of Blister fly.		斑蝥膏
„	Catechu and alum.	兒茶白礬膏
„	Chalk.	石粉膏
„	Iodine.	挨阿顚膏
„	Galls and opium.	沒石子鴉片膏
„	Sugar of lead.	鉛散膏
„	Mercury or blue ointment.	水銀濃黑膏
„	Mercury, diluted.	水銀淡黑膏
„	Red oxide of mercury.	水銀紅膏
„	Nitrate of mercury—citrine.	水銀黃膏
„	Nitrate of silver or caustic.	各息的膏
„	Sulphate of copper.	膽礬膏
„	Resin.	松香膏
„	Sulphur.	硫黃膏
„	Tartar—emetic.	吐吐伊蜜的膏
„	White wax.	白臘膏
„	Yellow wax.	黃臘膏
Verdigris.		銅綠
Vinegar.		醋

Zinc, sulphate of, or vomiting powder. 精錡嘔散

PROPERTIES OF MEDICINES. 藥之功力

Aperient.	輕瀉
Alterative.	解血毒
Antispasmodic.	安肚腹腦氣筋
Antidote.	解食物毒
Antilithic.	解溺中沙粉
Anthelmintic.	殺蟲
Astringent.	收歛
Carminative.	去風
Cathartic.	重瀉
Counter-irritants.	引病外出
Demulcent.	潤腸胃內皮
Diuretic.	利小便
Diaphoretic.	發汗
Disinfectant.	解病人毒氣
Emmenagogue.	調經
Emetic.	嘔吐
Emollient.	潤外皮
Escharotic.	令皮肉爛
Errhine.	取嚏
Laxative.	微利
Narcotic.	止病令寐
Refrigerant.	解熱
Rubefaciant.	令皮熱
Sialogogue.	生口津
Sedative.	平火安心
Stimulant.	補精神即補火

Stomachic.	開胃 暖胃
Tonic.	補血力

OPERATIONS IN PHARMACY. 炮製之法

Distilling.	蒸汽
Filtering.	濾渣
Clarifying.	澄清
Expressing.	榨壓
Decocting or boiling.	熬煮
Fusing or melting.	銷鍊
Infusing.	冲泡
Pulverising.	研末
Sifting.	篩細
Mixing.	和合
Macerating in water.	水浸
Macerating in spirit.	酒浸
Evaporating or drying.	烘曬

WEIGHTS AND MEASURES. 稱藥之器

Large and small scales.	大小天秤
Money or grain scales.	釐戥
Chinese weights.	中國權法
16 leang, a catty.	十六兩爲一斤
8 leang, a half catty.	八兩爲半斤
10 tseen, a leang.	十錢爲一兩
10 fun or candareens, a tseen.	十分爲一錢
5 candareens, a half tseen.	五分爲半錢
10 le, a candareen.	十釐爲一分
English and Chinese weights.	英華權法

...und equal to twelve leang.		十二兩爲一磅子
...pound	„ six leang.	六兩爲半磅子
...achms	„ one leang.	英十錢中一兩等重
...nce	„ eight tseen.	英一昻子中八錢等重
...unce	„ four tseen.	英半昻子中四錢等重
...achm	„ one tseen.	英一錢中一錢等重
...achm	„ five fun.	英半錢中半錢等重
...rains	„ one fun and a half.	英十釐中一分半等重
...rains	„ seven le and a half.	英五釐中七釐有餘
...grains	„ four le and a half.	英三釐中五釐不足
...rains	„ about three le.	英二釐中三釐等重
...al pint	„ sixteen leang.	英二十水昻子中一斤
...id ounces „	eight leang.	英十水昻子中八兩重
...id ounces „	four leang.	英五水昻子中四兩重

ELEMENTS OF NATURAL SCIENCE. 博物之理

...e property of bodies.	物質物性
...may be changed, but not des-oyed.	物質變不能滅盡
...has cohesive attraction.	物有牽合之性
...also the property of repulsion.	物亦有推拒之性
...is a mutual affinity in bodies.	物質同者喜牽合
...attract and unite with metal.	金質牽合金質
...or aqueous bodies, attract water.	水質牽引水質
...aeriform bodies, attract air.	氣質牽引氣質
...wer of attraction is great or small.	牽引力有大有小
...n attracts the earth.	日牽引地球
...rth attracts the moon.	地球牽引月輪
...oon attracts the tides.	月牽引潮水
...rth attracts every thing to itself.	地牽引附地諸物

Bodies gravitate to the earth not from it. 物向地不能離地

Bodies are at rest or in motion. 物動靜二性

Rapid motion cannot instantly cease. 動極不能即止

Nor can bodies at rest, be put into motion at once. 靜者不能即動

Inertia and momentum are antagonistic. 靜動之力勝負相對

Rapid motion quickly checked is dangerous. 動極驟止則傷

A horse stopping suddenly, the rider falls forward. 馳馬驟止人仆前

Or moving suddenly, the rider falls backward. 馬驟馳人仆後

Collision injures according to the rate of motion. 兩物撞觸動速者傷多

The Atmosphere. 地球周圍之氣

Its height is about 150 Chinese le. 地氣上升百五十里

The higher it is from the earth, the lighter it becomes. 氣離地面愈遠愈輕

The atmosphere is composed of oxygen and nitrogen. 養氣淡氣合爲地氣

From supporting life, it is called vital air. 生物倚賴故稱生氣

The two gases are blended in fixed proportions. 養氣淡氣調和有定度

Oxygen is so called from its nourishing qualities. 養育萬類稱養氣

Nitrogen simply dilutes the oxygen. 淡氣淡養氣之用

In 1000 parts of air there is one of carbon. 生氣千分炭氣一分

Carbon is emitted in expiration. 肺呼出炭氣

It is also the result of combustion. 物焚燒出炭氣

Inspiring only carbon would be fatal. 獨吸炭氣則死

Vegetation (on the contrary) lives upon it 植物借炭氣而生

In the air there is also aqueous vapour. 生氣中有水汽

It is most abundant in hot damp weather. 天熱雨多則汽多

At night it is condensed & forms dew. 水汽夜遇冷爲露

...tmospheric pressure.	地氣有壓重之力
...rts mercury to the height of 28 ...ches.	托高管內水銀廿八英寸
...vater to the height of 32 feet.	托高管內水卅二英尺
...r presses equally in all directions.	地氣壓力周圍勻同
...s therefore unconscious of its ...eight.	壓力勻故人不覺
...ir in rapid motion is wind.	地氣速動謂之風
...ength corresponds to its motion.	風大小依氣動遲速
...eat of the sun causes the air to ...scend.	地氣受日熱則上升
...air immediately supplies its place	隨時有氣補空缺
...the equator north and south are ...e trades.	近赤道南北為恒信風
...ir-pump.	抽風之器名氣機筩
...ound glass cylinder.	器上用玻璃圓罩
...mp empties the air in the cylinder.	機筩抽出罩內之氣
...iving thing within, then dies.	納生物於罩內則死
...terfly is unable to fly.	納蝶於罩內則不飛
...ted candle is extinguished.	納火於罩內即滅
... gives out no sound.	納鈴於罩內無聲
...owder will not ignite.	納火藥於罩內不燒
... and a feather fall together.	罩內無氣錢毛齊落
...arometer.	風雨針
...ercury is placed in a tube.	水銀貯玻璃管內
...air enters it is useless.	外氣泄入則不應
...ercury rises in fine weather.	水銀升則晴霽
... indicates bad weather.	水銀降則風雨
...anges depend on atmospheric ...ressure.	升降依地氣壓力
...len fall indicates a storm.	水銀忽降有大風雨
...riners and farmers it is most ...luable.	海客農夫此為至寶

The Thermometer.	寒暑針
Both ends of a glass tube are closed.	玻璃管口兩端皆閉
The mercury is in the bulb.	管底有膽貯水銀
It contracts and expands according to the temperature.	水銀寒縮熱漲
As it expands it rises, and vice versa.	漲則升縮則降
A table indicates the degrees.	玻璃管旁號識度分
32 is the freezing point.	英以三十二度爲冰點
60 to 70 neither hot nor cold.	六七十度寒暑適中
96 blood or great heat.	人血本熱九十六度
110 fever heat.	熱病一百十度
212 the boiling point.	沸湯熱二百十二度

Hydrogen or light gas.	輕氣
Air-balloon.	輕氣球
Hydrogen is much lighter than air.	輕氣比地氣輕數倍
Carburetted hydrogen or coal gas.	炭氣輕氣卽煤炭氣
The safety lamp prevents explosion.	煤窯燈籠隔毒氣不焚

Heat and light are imponderable.	熱與光不能權稱
There are six kinds of heat.	熱分六等
Natural or solar heat.	日熱
Fire or artificial heat.	火熱
Electric or galvanic heat.	電氣熱
Animal heat.	肉身熱卽本熱
Heat from chemical changes.	化成熱
Heat from friction.	二物相擊熱
All bodies have their own natural heat.	各物皆有本熱
They also receive and radiate heat.	物能接熱能傳散熱
Heat is radiated equally in all directions.	熱必傳散周勻
There are good and bad radiators of heat.	物質傳散有難易

Those that receive it easily radiate it easily.	接熱易者出熱亦易
All metals are good conductors of heat.	五金傳熱最易
Wood, stone, glass, are bad conductors.	木石玻璃傳熱難
Bright and smooth surfaces reflect heat	物瑩滑能返照熱
Rough and black surfaces readily absorb it.	物粗礪色黑接熱易
Bodies are either solid, fluid, or aeriform.	物分實質水質氣質
The natural heat of each is different.	三質本熱不同
Solids by increase of heat may be changed into fluids.	實質添熱變爲水質
Fluids also into gases.	水質添熱變爲氣質
Every thing is expanded by heat.	物得熱則發大
The vapor of boiling water is steam.	沸湯變氣稱蒸汽
The property of steam is expansive.	蒸汽性散而不聚
When confined its expansive power is very great.	蒸汽被束則力極大
Heat adds to its power.	汽加火熱力更大
Steam power is extensively employed.	汽力之用甚大
It is the moving power of the steamer.	汽力運行火輪船
And the steam engine or locomotive.	汽力運行火輪車

Solar light.	日光
It travels with immense velocity.	光行至速無物可比
In a direct or straight course.	光直射
It is deflected by water or glass.	光透玻璃清水斜射
Like heat it may be reflected.	光能返照
The moon is reflected light.	月光係日光返照
A prism decomposes solar light.	日光透三角鏡分七色
White or colourless light is the union of seven tints.	日光七色合爲白
Heat always accompanies solar light.	日熱常與日光並行
It is found in the red coloured ray.	日熱寓於紅光內
Colour of objects is reflected light.	各物色係日光返

Black is the absorption of all the tints.	物全接日光則色黑
White is the entire reflection of them.	物不接日光則色白
The rainbow.	虹霓
The rain in sun shine acts like a prism.	日之光透雨成虹霓
The telescope.	大小千里鏡
The microscope.	大小顯微鏡
The camera.	收景鏡
A concave lens.	凹鏡
A convex lens.	凸鏡
The former causes light to diverge.	凹鏡透光令光展開
The latter brings it to a focus.	凸鏡透光成尖樞
Electricity.	電氣
Electrical machine.	電機器
The loadstone.	攝石
The magnet.	攝鐵
Magnetic wire.	電氣傳鐵線有攝力
The compass.	指南盤
The indicator or needle.	指南針
Electricity of the earth.	地體之電氣
Electricity of the clouds.	天雲之電氣
Electric state undisturbed.	電氣和則靜
Electric state excited.	電氣不和則亂動
The electric fluids are negative and positive.	電氣具陰陽二性
When separated they strongly attract each other.	陰陽離必牽引復合
Concussion of electric clouds is thunder.	電氣在雲中觸擊爲雷
Lightning is the electric flash.	閃係電氣所射之火光
Thunder is harmless, lightning dangerous.	殺人非雷是電火
It is most dangerous when they are together.	閃電雷聲齊發最危